Odd One Out

WILD ANIMALS

Alix Wood

WINDMILL BOOKS ™

Published in 2023 by Windmill Books,
an Imprint of Rosen Publishing
2544 Clinton St.
Buffalo, NY 14224

Produced for Rosen Publishing by Alix Wood Books
Designed by Alix Wood
Edited by Eloise Macgregor
Editor for Rosen: Kerri O'Donnell

Photo credits:
All images © Shutterstock; or in the public domain, with grateful thanks to the photographers who allowed them to be creative commons

Printed in the United States of America

CPSIA Compliance Information: Batch CWWM23
For Further Information contact Rosen Publishing at 1-800-237-9932

Cataloging-in-Publication Data

Names: Wood, Alix.
Title: Wild animals / Alix Wood.
Description: New York : Windmill Books, 2023. | Series: Odd one out | Includes answer key.
Identifiers: ISBN 9781538392676 (pbk) | ISBN 9781538392683 (library bound) | ISBN 9781538392690 (ebook)
Subjects: LCSH: Wild animals--Juvenile literature
Classification: LCC QL49 W66 2023 | DDC 590--dc23

Find us on

Can you find the odd one out? It's not always that easy!

The answers are on page 24

Which one is not ...

a bear?

Can you spot who ...

is not a leopard?

Which animal is not ...

a deer?

Who is not a tiger?

Which one is not ...

a monkey?

Can you see who ...

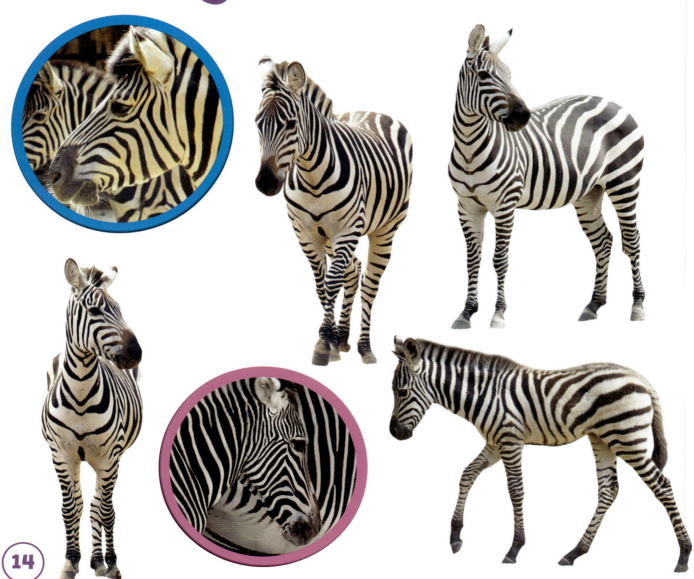

is not a zebra?

Who is not an elephant?

One of these is ...

not a lion.

Which animal is not ...

a rhinoceros?

Find who isn't ...

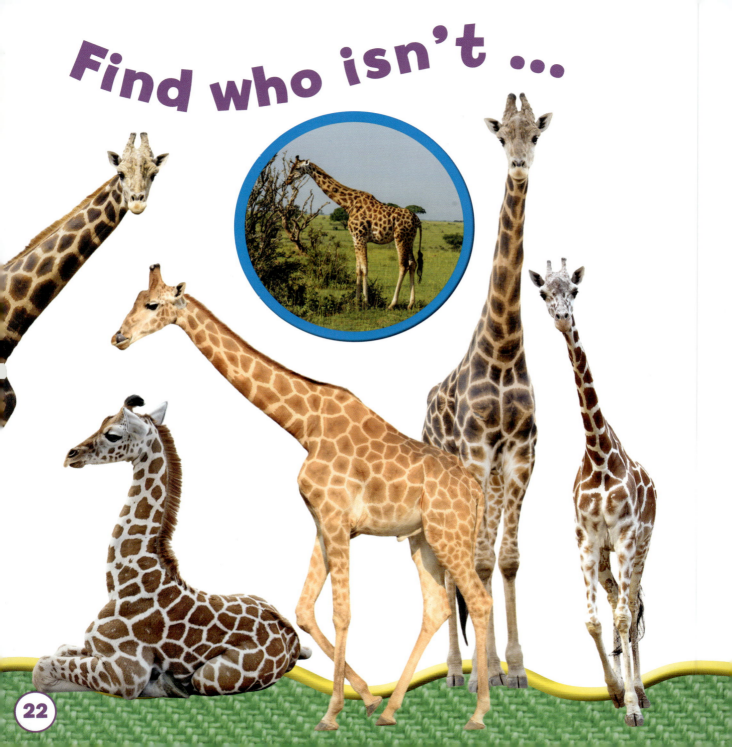

a giraffe.